Sleepy Little Mouse

For Kim and Matthew, who didn't want to have a nap — E. F.
For Robyn, who loves to have a nap — K. F.

Text © 2000 Eugenie Fernandes
Illustrations © 2000 Kim Fernandes
Photography by Pat Lacroix

Kids Can Press acknowledges the financial support of the Ontario Arts Council, the Canada Council for the Arts and the Government of Canada, through the BPIDP, for our publishing activity.

Published in Canada by
Kids Can Press Ltd.
29 Birch Avenue
Toronto, ON M4V 1E2

Published in the U.S. by
Kids Can Press Ltd.
2250 Military Road
Tonawanda, NY 14150

www.kidscanpress.com

The artwork in this book was rendered in Fimo®, a pliable modeling material.
The text is set in Avenir.

Edited by Debbie Rogosin
Designed by Julia Naimska
Printed in Hong Kong by Wing King Tong Company Limited

The hardcover edition of this book is smyth sewn casebound.
The paperback edition of this book is limp sewn with a drawn-on cover.

CM 00 0 9 8 7 6 5 4 3 2 1
CM PA 02 0 9 8 7 6 5 4 3 2 1

National Library of Canada Cataloguing in Publication Data

Fernandes, Eugenie, 1943–
Sleepy little mouse

ISBN 1-55074-701-0 (bound)   ISBN 1-55074-703-7 (pbk.)

I. Fernandes, Kim II. Title.

PS8561.E7596S53 2000   jC813'.54   C99-932927-8
PZ7.F47SI 2000

Kids Can Press is a Nelvana company

Sleepy Little Mouse

Written by **Eugenie Fernandes**
Illustrated by **Kim Fernandes**

KIDS CAN PRESS

Once upon a time there was a little mouse who was so tired that her mommy took her to her room to have a nap. But the little mouse didn't want to have a nap, so she began to cry.

Her mommy kissed her and tucked in her covers. But the sleepy little mouse kicked off her covers and cried some more.

The little mouse's mommy read her a story and sang her a song. "Now close your eyes and have a nice nap," she said.

But the little mouse didn't want to have a nice nap. She wanted to play. So she cried some more.

Finally, her mommy said, "Sleep tight," and she left the room.

The sleepy little mouse cried and cried until her tears filled the room and her bed began to float around.

She cried until her bed floated right out the window and down to the river and out to sea. And the little mouse kept on crying.

She cried until all the birds and all the fish and all the creatures from the sea came to find out what was going on.

"I don't want to have a nice nap," said the little mouse. "I want to play."

So, all the birds and all the fish
and all the creatures from the sea
played with the little mouse.

Under the covers and over the waves, on and on they played — until the little mouse, who really was very tired, lay down and closed her eyes. The birds and the fish and the creatures from the sea sang her a lovely song and the little mouse fell fast asleep.

When her mommy heard her fall
asleep, she got into her boat and
sailed out the window and down
to the river and out to sea to where
her little mouse was sleeping.

She whispered, "I love you," and towed her back to her very own room …

where the little mouse had
a wonderful nap.